This book is dedicated to our little princess, Kenzie. You may be gone but you will live in our hearts and in these books.

Love you always and forever, mommy, daddy, Max and Zac.

By Stephanie Pyles
Illustrated by Maru Salem-Vargas

Kenzie and Bun Bun

First Dance Class

By Stephanie Pyles

Illustrated by Maru Salem–Vargas

Hi, I'm Kenzie. This is my friend Bun Bun. A lot of people say I'm nonverbal. I can talk, I just choose not to.

I find fun and creative ways to express what I'm feeling or what I want.

For now I only say a few words. Maybe one day
I will say more. These are our adventures!

Today is a big day.
Today is Kenzie's first
dance class.
But first, she must run
errands with her mama.

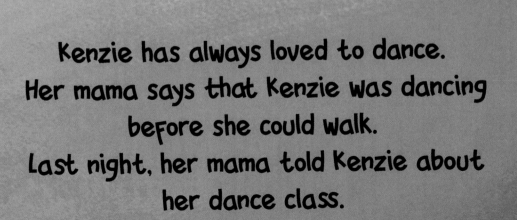

Kenzie has always loved to dance.
Her mama says that Kenzie was dancing
before she could walk.
Last night, her mama told Kenzie about
her dance class.

Kenzie's mama told her she was going to meet her new dance teacher, Ms. T.
She couldn't wait to meet her new friends and learn new things.

Mama told her that she would be doing ballet AND tap class.
Kenzie tried putting on her shoes to make sure they still fit.

Oh no. Kenzie's shoes didn't fit her anymore.
Mama told Kenzie her feet must have grown overnight.
They both laughed.

So today, one of their stops is to buy new shoes for dance.
Yum. Yum. Strawberry syrup is Kenzie's favorite.
After they eat, they'll start their adventure.

At the salon, Kenzie's mama gets
her hair dyed pink.
Her mama always has fun colors
in her hair.

Kenzie is getting her nails painted.
She picked pink, too.

At the bakery, Kenzie gets to pick out cookies for her new dance teacher, Ms. T.
"Which cookies do you think she'll want, Kenzie?" asks her mama.

Kenzie points to..
SNICKERDOODLES!

TIPPY.

At the dance store, Kenzie gets to pick out
her own shoes.

TAP. TAP.

Kenzie walks around the floor making sure the shoes now fit.
She loves to hear the sound her new shoes make.

Finally at dance. Kenzie is super excited.
With the biggest smile on her face, she waves at the other
children in the room.

She dances in a circle with her new dance friends.
They all laugh as they hold hands.

Kenzie doesn't follow what the teacher is saying. She is following the beat of her own feet.

She leaps across the floor.
With practice, she'll get better.

Five, six, seven, eight..
She points her toes along to the beat.
After all the new fun, it is time to go.

At home, after a day of fun... Kenzie realizes that something is missing.

Oh no. Bun Bun isn't here.
Bun Bun is missing.

"It's okay, Kenzie. We will go back out and find Bun Bun," her mama says.
But Kenzie thinks that something bad will happen to Bun Bun.

What if he gets swept up with the hair?

Wooosh!

What if he gets made into a cake?

What if he's thrown out with the trash?

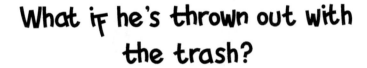

What if another girl takes him home?

No, he isn't at the salon.

He isn't at the bakery.

Not at the dance store, either.

Oh where, oh where, can Bun Bun be?

This is their last stop, and Kenzie is sad.
She worries she'll never see Bun Bun again.
Kenzie finally looks up.

And what does she see?
Bun Bun sitting patiently.

"Bun Bun danced a bit while he waited for you," Ms. T says with a smile.

Kenzie thanks her mama with the biggest hug.
They found him!
He is safe in her arms again.

At home, it is time for dinner.
Spaghetti, another favorite.
She loves slurping up the long noodles.
Slurp, slurp, slurp.

As she slurps up a noodle, Kenzie wonders
what type of adventure her and Bun Bun will
go on tomorrow.
She couldn't wait.

AUTHOR'S ACKNOWLEDGEMENTS

I would like to thank everyone who purchased this book. I wrote it to honor my daughter, who sadly passed away at the age of three. My mission is to spread joy and happiness. I want to show the world just how special my little girl truly was.

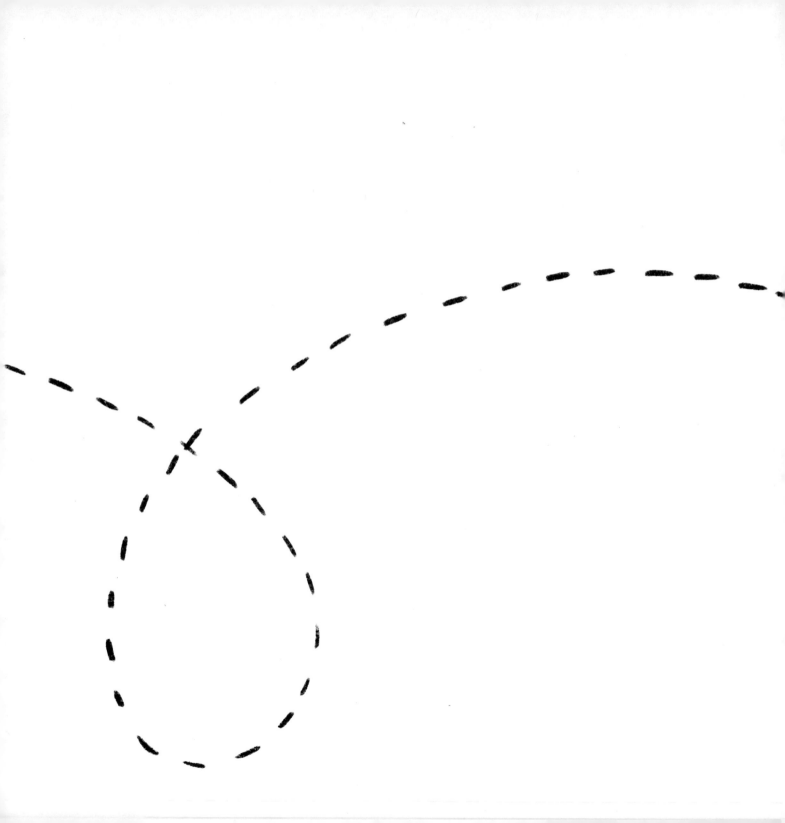

Made in the USA
Middletown, DE
23 September 2022

11115645R00020